For my mom, Rose D. Slonim,

with special thanks to
Jonathan, Daniel, Michael and Mary Slonim,
and Susan Pearson

Book design by Kristen M. Nobles and David Slonim.
Typeset in Centaur and Providence Sans.
The illustrations in this book were rendered in reed pen and ink
and watercolors on Arches 140-pound watercolor paper.
Manufactured in China.

Library of Congress Cataloging-in-Publication Data
Slonim, David.
Oh, Ducky! / by David Slonim.
p. cm.
Summary: Johnny, who works at a chocolate factory, loses his beloved rubber ducky
in the chocolate machine, but with help from a music-loving taste tester
and a nutty inventor, everything comes out just fine.
ISBN 0-8118-3562-6
[1. Toys—Fiction. 2. Factories—Fiction. 3. Candy—Fiction.
4. Chocolate—Fiction.] I. Title.
PZ7.S6338 Oh 2003
[Fic]—dc21
2002005339

Distributed in Canada by Raincoast Books
9050 Shaughnessy Street, Vancouver, British Columbia V6P 6E5

10 9 8 7 6 5 4 3 2 1

Chronicle Books LLC
85 Second Street, San Francisco, California 94105

www.chroniclekids.com

Oh, Ducky!

A Chocolate Calamity by David Slonim

chronicle books · san francisco

This is Mr. Peters.

BANG!

Ahhhhhh!

Mr. Peters likes
to build useful gadgets.

Mr. Peters drives a truck.

A CANDY truck!

He makes the candy
at his chocolate factory.

This is Johnny.

Johnny likes to be helpful.

Johnny works the candy machine at the factory.
He loves his job almost as much as he loves
his rubber duck.

And this is Pauline.
Pauline loves music.

She also loves her job at the chocolate factory.
Pauline is in charge of Quality Control.

One day, as Johnny struggled
to fix a leaky valve,

Boink!

the machine

stopped

making

candy.

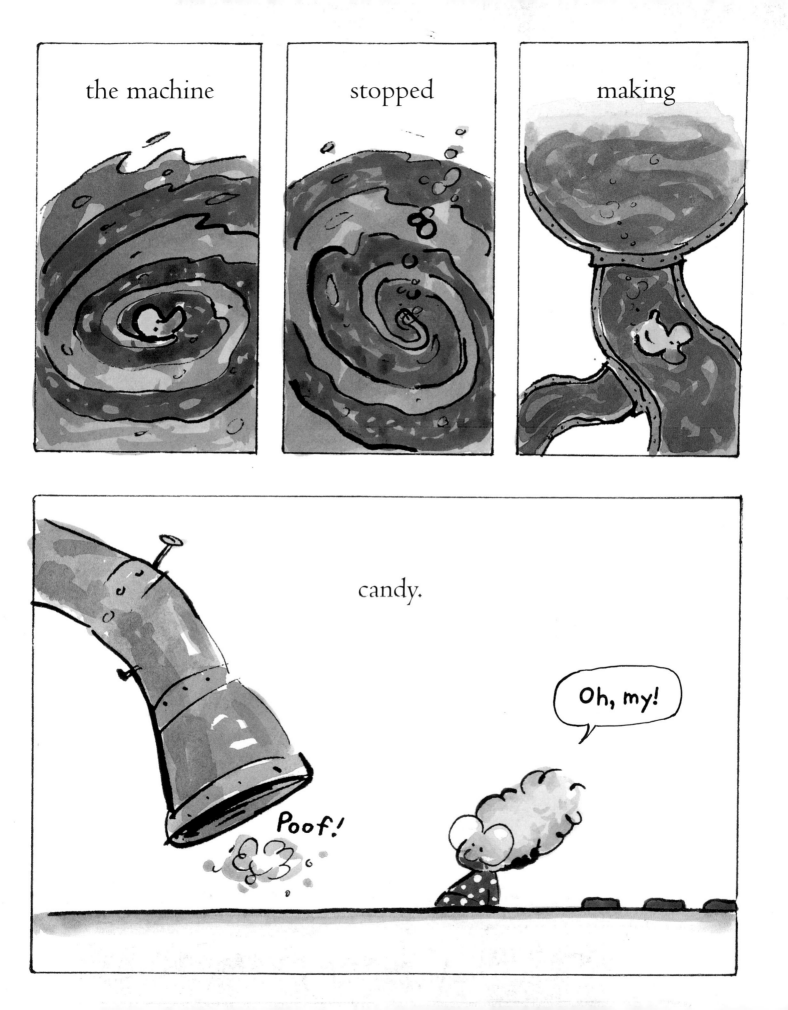

"I'm going in!" declared Mr. Peters.
Pauline and Johnny gasped.
They begged him not to risk it.
"Suit me up!" said Mr. Peters.

They lowered Mr. Peters into the chocolate machine

and waited.

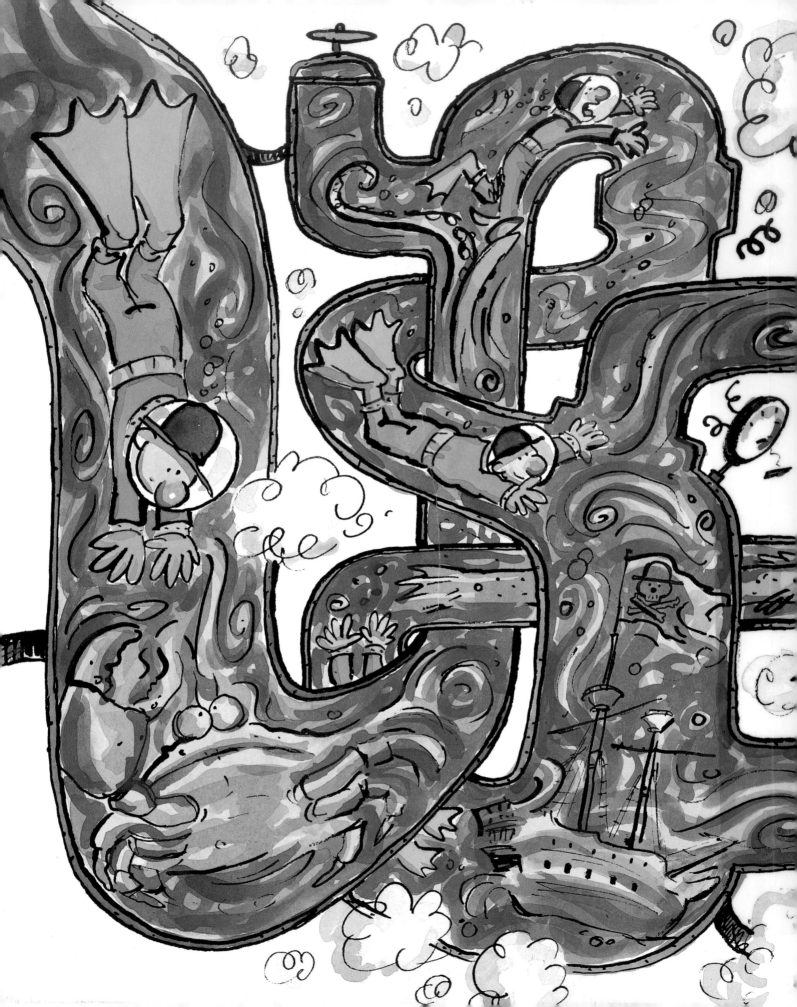

"Look!" said Pauline.
"Oh, Ducky!" said Johnny. "Squeak to me!"
"Oh, Johnny," said Pauline,
"Mr. Peters will be furious."

But Mr. Peters wasn't angry at all.
Mr. Peters was inspired.

They all worked hard to bring the big idea to life.
Finally it was ready.

And so does everyone else!